THOMAS and the Big, Big Bridge

Illustrated by Tom LaPadula and Paul Lopez

A GOLDEN BOOK • NEW YORK

Thomas the Tank Engine & Friends

A BRITT ALLCROFT COMPANY PRODUCTION

Based on The Railway Series by The Rev. W. Awdry
Copyright © Gullane (Thomas) LLC 2001
All rights reserved under International and Pan-American Copyright Conventions. Published in the United States by
Golden Books, an imprint of Random House Children's Books, a division of Random House, Inc., New York, and
simultaneously in Canada by Random House of Canada Limited, Toronto. Originally published in slightly different form by
Random House, Inc., in 2001. Golden Books, A Golden Book, A Little Golden Book, the G colophon, and the distinctive
gold spine are registered trademarks of Random House, Inc.
www.randomhouse.com/kids   www.goldenbooks.com   www.thomasthetankengine.com
Library of Congress Control Number: 2002108479
ISBN: 0-307-10335-8
PRINTED IN USA   First Random House edition 2003
20 19 18 17 16 15 14 13 12

It was a special day for the railway!

"We are here to launch the new rail line through the Mountains of Sodor," Sir Topham Hatt announced. "Today we open the big, big bridge!"

What wonderful news! Everyone cheered. The mountains were beautiful. The people of Sodor couldn't wait to visit them.

Everyone wanted to see the big, big bridge. It had towers so high the tops touched the sky. And the valley beneath was so deep that when you were on the big, big bridge, you could barely see the ground.

Thomas was excited about the new rail line.
"This really is a special day!" he said happily.
Then Henry chugged up to Thomas. The big engine frowned.

"I don't want to go to the mountains," Henry said nervously. "It's windy up there—very, very windy." Henry didn't like the wind. Henry didn't like rain or snow or hail, either.

"You're a big engine, Henry!" Thomas said. "You shouldn't be afraid of a little wind."

But Henry was afraid. And that made Thomas a bit afraid, too.

"Gordon! Henry! Thomas! Hitch up your coaches!" called Sir Topham Hatt. "It's time for your first trip to the mountains."

Percy and James were glad they didn't have to go to the mountains. They were afraid to cross the big, big bridge, too.

"There's nothing to be afraid of," Thomas insisted, in a voice loud enough for Percy and James to hear. "It will be easy to cross the big, big bridge."

Thomas and Henry chugged to the platform. Gordon the Express Engine was already there. His coaches were full of passengers.

Annie and Clarabel were soon hitched behind Thomas. "Hurry, hurry," they called.

"All aboard!" cried the conductor.

Sir Topham Hatt turned to the crowd and waved his hat one last time.

Toot, toot, Gordon whistled. "Follow me!"

In a burst of steam, the big blue engine was off.

Soon the trains were rolling through the countryside in a long line. Gordon took the lead. Behind him chugged Henry. Then, because he was the smallest, came Thomas.

All along the way, people came out of their houses and cheered when they saw the trains go by.

At the foot of the mountain, Henry slowed to a crawl. "These mountains are much too high," he moaned. "I *can't* go. I'm afraid of heights!"

"Don't be silly," said Thomas bravely. "I'll be right here behind you."

But Henry didn't budge. He was very nervous. And that made Thomas nervous, too.

"Come on!" Thomas gently pushed Henry. "We have to go!"

The brand-new tracks were smooth and shiny, but Henry barely moved along them. The truth was, Henry didn't want to reach the top of the mountain, because then he'd have to cross the big, big bridge.

"If Percy and James and Henry are all afraid," thought Thomas, "maybe *I* should be frightened, too!"

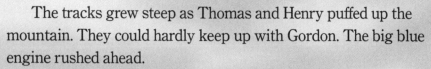

The tracks grew steep as Thomas and Henry puffed up the mountain. They could hardly keep up with Gordon. The big blue engine rushed ahead.

Gordon was a strong engine. The steep tracks didn't tire him at all!

"Wait for us!" Henry called. But Gordon climbed higher and higher, until he was out of sight.

"I don't think I can make it," Henry groaned, his steam giving out at last. "This mountain is too steep!"

"Keep going!" Thomas urged him. "We can't let a little mountain stop us."

But Thomas was having trouble chugging up the steep mountain, too. And he was beginning to worry about crossing the big, big bridge.

Finally, Thomas and Henry arrived at the top of the mountain.
There it was—the big, big bridge! And it was high. It was windy
up there, too—*very* windy.

"I won't go," Henry declared.

"But we have to cross!" Thomas said bravely. "Our passengers want to see the mountains on the other side."

"Hurry, hurry!" Annie and Clarabel cried. The coaches were so excited that Thomas had trouble keeping them in line.

Thomas searched the tracks ahead. Gordon was nowhere to be seen. He had already crossed the bridge and rolled into the mountains beyond.

Thomas and Henry were alone.

"I'll go first," Thomas said at last. "Then you can follow me, Henry."

"If the wind blows, close your eyes," Henry said. "That way you won't see anything scary."

Click-clack! Click-clack! Click-clack! Thomas began to cross the bridge.

Thomas looked up. He could see cottony clouds touching the top of the bridge.

Nervously, he looked down. But the bridge was so high he couldn't see the ground.

A sudden gust of wind shook the bridge. This scared Thomas, and he closed his eyes so tightly that he couldn't see where he was going.

Click-clack! Click-clack! Click-CRASH! Thomas came to a sudden stop. He opened one eye for a quick peek. "Oh, no!" he cried. His wheels were off the track!

"Are you all right, Thomas?" called Henry.

"I'm stuck," Thomas said glumly. "I couldn't see where I was going and my front wheels have jumped the track."

Just then, Gordon returned. He frowned when he saw Thomas stuck in the middle of the bridge.

"Go find Harold," Gordon called to Henry. Relieved, Henry backed
down the mountain to find the helicopter.

Thomas kept his eyes closed. He was too afraid to look. But
inside his coaches, the passengers enjoyed the wonderful view.

Finally, Thomas heard the whirl of rotors. Harold was here to rescue him!

Slowly, Thomas opened his eyes. He looked at the blue sky above and the green mountains all around.

"What a lovely view!" he exclaimed. "I was silly to shut my eyes. I almost missed everything."

"Hitch the rope to your buffer and hold on!" Harold cried.

In no time at all, Harold had lifted Thomas back onto the tracks.
Thomas backed up to where Henry waited.

"Come on, Henry," said Thomas. "The view is spectacular.
I should never have been afraid."

With that, Thomas turned and chugged happily across the big,
big bridge. Henry watched in wonder.

"If *he's* not afraid, maybe I shouldn't be, either!" Henry decided.

Slowly, the big green engine made his way across the bridge, too.

Soon Thomas and Henry arrived at the station house. The mountains were really lovely. Everyone was happy to have seen them. But Thomas was the happiest one of all.

He was proud that he had crossed the big, big bridge!